Mandragora s.r.l.
piazza del Duomo 9
50122 Firenze
www.mandragora.it

Text
Sandra Rosi, after Collodi's *Pinocchio*

Editing, design and typesetting
Michèle Fantoli, Marco Salucci, Paola Vannucchi

English translation
Catherine Bolton

Printed in Italy by Alpilito, Firenze
Bound by Legatoria LET, Campi Bisenzio

isbn 978-88-7461-183-6

Read&Work

Pinocchio

illustrated by Silvia Serafini

Mandragora

One fine day a piece of wood was delivered
to the shop of a carpenter everyone called Master
Cherry because his nose was as red as a cherry.
Master Cherry started to carve it to make a table leg,
but was astonished to discover
that the block of wood could speak!
Frightened, he decided to give it to his friend
Geppetto, who just happened to arrive
at that very moment to ask
for a piece of wood
so he could carve a marionette.

Back home, Geppetto started to work
on his marionette and decided to call it Pinocchio.
The minute he started carving the eyes,
nose and mouth, he noticed that Pinocchio
was observing him, laughing
and making faces.
But, above all,
his nose grew
and grew and grew.
Yet there was
more in store
for Geppetto,
because
as soon as he
finished carving
the figure, Pinocchio
stretched his legs
and dashed out
the front door.

Geppetto ran after him shouting "Grab him! Grab him!" to everyone he encountered along the way, but people simply stared at the fleeing marionette and burst out laughing. Luckily, a carabineer arrived, attracted by all the ruckus, and he grabbed Pinocchio by his long nose.

However, the passers-by started saying that Geppetto was a bad man and that the marionette had been right to run away from home. Therefore, the carabineer freed Pinocchio and put poor Geppetto in jail!

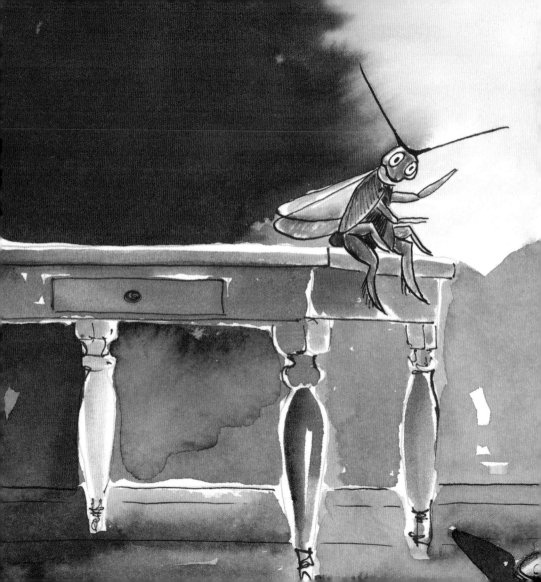

Pinocchio went home, where he found
a Talking Cricket who wanted to reveal
a great truth to him:
"Woe to children who rebel against their
parents, don't go to school and don't
learn a trade, because they always
end up in hospital or prison."

Pinocchio, who
instead wanted to be
a vagabond, told him to hold
his tongue and, losing his temper,
he hurled a wooden mallet
at the Talking Cricket,
killing him instantly.

Night fell and Pinocchio suddenly felt very hungry. Therefore, he decided to go out into the cold to beg for a piece of bread, but a farmer who did not want to be disturbed threw a bucket of icy water over him. The marionette started to cry because he was all alone without his father. Shivering and hungry, he went home, set his feet on the hot embers to dry and promptly fell asleep. While he slept, his feet—made of wood—began to burn and turned to ashes.

In the morning,

Geppetto came home and gave
the famished marionette the three pears
he had set aside for his own breakfast.
Fussy at first, Pinocchio refused to touch
the peel or the core, but in the end he
was so hungry that he ate every last bite.
The poor man refashioned Pinocchio's
burnt feet and, out of gratitude,
the marionette said he
would go to school.
Geppetto, who didn't have
a penny in his pocket,
made him a suit
of flowered paper,
a pair of shoes from tree
bark and a cap from
bread dough. Then,
although it was snowing,
he sold his only coat to buy
Pinocchio a spelling book.

Carrying his new spelling book,
Pinocchio was walking to school
when he heard the sound of pipes
and a bass drum.

Forgetting all his good intentions,
he ran towards the music
and found himself in the middle
of a crowd before a marionette
theatre called Gran Teatro
dei Burattini.
Overcome with curiosity, he sold
his spelling book for four pennies
and used the money
to buy a ticket to the show.
Inside the theatre, the marionettes
recognized him and called him
to the stage, where they started
to laugh and joke with him,
stopping the show
and enraging the audience.

Furious about the commotion, the terrible show director, named Fire Eater, grabbed Pinocchio to use him to stoke the fire over which he was roasting his supper, but when the marionette started to cry, he was moved and decided to spare him.

After hearing his story, Fire Eater felt so sorry for the marionette that he gave him five gold coins to buy poor Geppetto a new coat.

On his way home, Pinocchio met the Fox and the Cat, two tricksters who convinced him to join them, making him believe that if he buried his coins in the Field of Miracles a tree laden with gold coins would grow overnight.

They walked and walked, and towards evening the exhausted trio arrived at a inn called Osteria del Gambero Rosso, where they stuffed themselves at Pinocchio's expense and then went to bed. When Pinocchio woke up in the middle of the night, he realized he was alone, and he dashed out to catch up with them.

On his way, Pinocchio turned around and, in the darkness, he saw two black figures wrapped in coal sacks. They were the Fox and the Cat who, disguised as assassins, started to chase him across the fields. Pinocchio, who hadn't recognized them, hid the coins in his mouth and ran off. But the two finally caught up with him and, to force him to spit out the coins, they hanged him from a great oak tree.

Living in a cottage in the woods was the beautiful Maiden with Azure Hair, a fairy who saw Pinocchio hanging from the tree, had him cut down and put him to bed. Then she called in three doctors, a Crow, an Owl and a Talking Cricket, to find out if he was dead or alive.

Pinocchio woke up and, although he had a terrible fever, he only agreed to take the bitter medicine when he saw that Black Rabbits were coming to take him away.

The Fairy then asked him how he had ended up in the hands of the assassins. Pinocchio responded with so many lies that his nose grew and grew to the point that he could no longer fit through the door.

The Fairy allowed the marionette to despair a while so would regret that he had lied to her.

She finally took pity on him and called the woodpeckers, which pecked at his long nose until it was back to its normal size. Pinocchio left to go to Geppetto, who was coming to get him, but on the road he encountered the Fox and the Cat again. After convincing him once more to bury his gold coins in the Field of Miracles, this time they managed to steal them and flee.

Pinocchio reported the theft, but was astonished to discover that he would be punished with four months in jail. Finally out of prison, he got caught in a trap set in a field where he had stopped to pick some grapes and was captured by a farmer. Thinking he was a chicken thief, the farmer forced Pinocchio to serve as his watchdog to guard the chicken coop in place of his dog Melampo, who had died that very day. When the real chicken thieves—weasels—arrived at night, Pinocchio barked like a dog, allowing the farmer to capture them. As a reward for his work, the man set him free and sent him on his way.

Pinocchio reached the seashore and, in the distance, saw Geppetto on a small boat being swallowed up by the sea. He dove in to save him, but a violent wave hurled him onto the Island of the Busy Bees. There he found the Fairy and promised her that he would become a good boy.
He started to attend school diligently until one day, during a angry brawl with his classmates, a classmate got hurt.
Pinocchio was wrongly blamed by the carabineers, but he ran into the sea, managing to escape their mastiff Alidoro and return home.

The Fairy had promised Pinocchio that she would turn him into a real boy like everyone else and that, for the occasion, she would throw a huge party.
The marionette dashed off to invite his friends, but Lampwick, the laziest of all, told him he wouldn't come because he was going to the Land of Toys, where there were no schools and children played all day.
So when Pinocchio saw the donkey-drawn wagon headed to that marvellous place, he didn't think twice and set off with his friend.

It was truly the land of plenty: the streets were lined with puppet theatres, and there were games and amusements everywhere. But after spending five months having fun, one morning Pinocchio awoke to discover that he had grown two large donkey ears.

He went straight to Lampwick, only to discover that the very same thing had happened to him. As they stared at each other they started to stagger and were ashamed to realize that they were turning into donkeys. They tried to cry and moan, but all they could do was bray!

"Ciuchino Pinocchio" the donkey was purchased by a stern circus director, who taught him to jump through hoops, and dance the waltz and the polka standing up on his hind legs. But on the evening of his debut, Pinocchio fell during a jump and sprained his leg.

As a result, he was sold for twenty coins to a man who wanted to use his skin to make a drumhead. The man tied a rock around Pinocchio and threw him in the water to drown.

At sea, fish gnawed

at Pinocchio the donkey, who turned back into a wooden marionette. However, a terrible Shark then swallowed him up whole. In the Shark's belly Pinocchio encountered a poor Tunny, waiting sadly to be digested. Continuing towards a feeble light in the distance he discovered Geppetto, who had survived in there for two years. Overjoyed, he convinced the old man to escape with him.

The Tunny, which thanks to Pinocchio also found its way out of the Shark's belly, helped the marionette and Geppetto get to shore. The two reached a hut and were finally safe. From then on, Pinocchio began to behave, working from morning to night to support his father. One day he learned that the Fairy was gravely ill. Therefore, he decided to give her the forty copper pennies he had saved. In reality, the Fairy had simply wanted to put his generosity to the test, so as a reward she gave him back gold coins in their stead. But, most importantly, she transformed him into a real boy at last. And the marionette?

Seated on a chair, his arms dangling limply, he constantly reminded the boy of how ridiculous he had once been.

Make your own Pinocchio

Required materials:
- blunt-tip scissors
- 8 paper fasteners

Cut out the parts
of the marionette
along the dotted lines.

Using a paper fastener, **punch holes**
in the dotted white circles.

Insert the paper fasteners through
the holes, connecting the holes that have
the same number, and flatten the wings
of the fasteners to secure them.

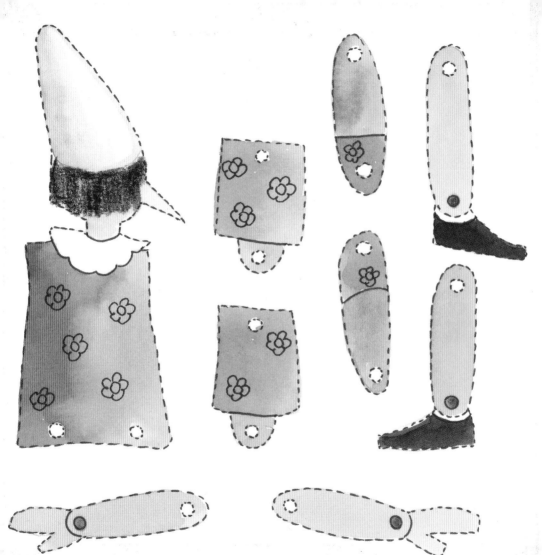